"Oh, Merrie, this is Rachel calling. Can you come down right now?"

A rustling in a hickory tree answered her.

"See her?" Rachel asked Toby.

Toby shook her head. "I see a hickory tree."

"Merrie, move closer," Rachel called. So Merrie flew down to a lower branch.

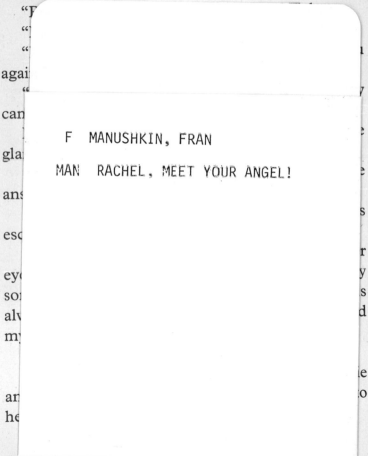

Rachel,
Meet Your Angel!

BY FRAN MANUSHKIN

PUFFIN BOOKS

Published by the Penguin Group
Penguin Books USA Inc., 375 Hudson Street, New York, New York 10014, U.S.A.
Penguin Books Ltd, 27 Wrights Lane, London W8 5TZ, England
Penguin Books Australia Ltd, Ringwood, Victoria, Australia
Penguin Books Canada Ltd, 10 Alcorn Avenue, Toronto, Ontario, Canada M4V 3B2
Penguin Books (N.Z.) Ltd, 182–190 Wairau Road, Auckland 10, New Zealand

Penguin Books Ltd, Registered Offices: Harmondsworth, Middlesex, England

First published in the United States of America by Puffin Books,
a division of Penguin Books USA Inc., 1995
Published by arrangement with Chardiet Unlimited, Inc.

1 3 5 7 9 10 8 6 4 2

LIBRARY OF CONGRESS CATALOGING-IN-PUBLICATION DATA

Manushkin, Fran.
Rachel, meet your angel! / by Fran Manushkin.
p.   cm.—(Angel Corners: #1)
Summary: After her father's death, Rachel and her mother move from Los
Angeles to the small town of Angel Corners, where she adjusts to her new life
with the help of some other fifth-grade girls and her very own guardian
angel.
ISBN 0-14-037198-2
[1. Guardian angels—Fiction. 2. Angels—Fiction. 3. Friendship—Fiction.]
I. Title. II. Series: Manushkin, Fran. Angel Corners; #1.
PZ7.M3195Rac 1995 [Fic]—dc20 94-34975 CIP AC

Printed in the United States of America
Set in Plantin

To Bernice Chardiet, who believed in me

CONTENTS

Rachel,
Meet Your Angel!

1

Do Angels Really Exist?

The first question tourists ask when they visit Angel Corners is "Where is the angel clock?" That's easy to answer. If you stroll along Main Street, you can't miss it. The clock is on the top of Town Hall, facing the village green.

The second question everyone asks is "Do angels really live here?" The answer is "Absolutely not!" They live in Heaven, but sometimes they come to visit. In fact, Zoe Mae, at the Angel Corners Sweet Shop, overheard an angel story the other day. Four girls who called themselves the Angel Club sat in a booth, talking about how an angel had recently changed their lives.

It all began a month ago on a peaceful, starry

night. If you had been on Hickory Hill that night, you would have seen a waterfall shimmering in the moonlight like an angel's wing. That's Angel Corners' famous Angel Falls.

As the waterfall bubbles along down the hill, it becomes Angel Stream, and passes the houses of all four girls in this story.

Valentine McCall, the most glamorous girl in fifth grade, was dreaming about marrying Zeb Burgess, the best-looking boy in school. But first, she would have to attract his attention!

Val's best friend, Lulu Bliss, was asleep in the apartment she shared with her father above his store, Starlight Video. Lulu was having a wild dream. She was directing her first movie, but the dinosaurs from *Jurassic Park* suddenly came leaping onto the set and one of them ate up her script!

Toby Antonio, a tall, athletic girl, was having an eventful dream that night, too. Wearing a pretty white tutu, she was dancing in the ballet *Sleeping Beauty*. Suddenly—tutu and all—she was on a basketball court, sinking the winning basket against the New York Knicks!

But there was one person in Angel Corners who was not dreaming that night. Rachel Summers, a girl with straight blond hair and dimples, was wide awake, trying hard not to cry.

Just that day, Rachel and her mother had moved

to Angel Corners. Partially unpacked boxes and open suitcases filled Rachel's small bedroom.

Gazing out the window at the first star to appear, Rachel made an impossible wish: "I wish Daddy were here." A few months ago, her father had run into the street to save a four-year-old boy from being hit by a car. The boy was saved—but Rachel's father had died.

Rachel missed her father so much. He had been such a warm, cheerful man. And he had adored Rachel. He always used to tell her she could do anything she set her mind to. Rachel had felt so safe and happy with her father. But now he was gone forever. Hugging her pillow, Rachel made her second impossible wish: "I wish I was back in our apartment in Los Angeles."

Rachel's father had grown up in Angel Corners, and had told wonderful stories about it. So when Rachel's mom had decided they should leave Los Angeles, with its sad memories, she thought of moving to Mr. Summers's hometown. Rachel's mom was a veterinarian, and it just so happened that Doc Wells, the Angel Corners vet, was retiring. Dr. Summers jumped at the chance to take his place.

"Whoo-whoo!" an owl called, and Rachel shivered. She was spooked by the night and the woods all around her house. Rachel closed her eyes tightly and tried to think of something cheerful. But all she

could think about was school tomorrow: Would the kids like her? Would she like her teacher?

The town clock began chiming the hour. Rachel counted along. The chimes passed twelve—going all the way to seventeen!

Rachel tried singing herself to sleep. She sang a lullaby she and her dad used to sing together. But Rachel's song was interrupted by a loud animal shriek in the woods. Rachel tugged her quilt over her head and burst into tears.

She had never felt so alone in her life.

But Rachel was not alone.

High in the starry sky someone with wise, kindly eyes was watching.

2

The Crystal Classroom

Florinda, the Queen of the Angels, was gazing down at Rachel. "Poor child." Florinda sighed. "She needs a guardian angel right away." Florinda was in the Crystal Classroom, at the Angel Academy, with her four angels-in-training.

"Send me! Oh, please send me!" they trilled, leaping out of their seats and flying around the room.

"Angels, please be seated!" Florinda urged. "I can't choose anyone with all this flurry!"

So Merribel, Serena, Amber, and Celeste flew back to their silver desks.

"Yikes!" Merrie cried out. "I keep forgetting to fold my wings when I sit down!" In truth, her wings did look a little the worse for wear.

Florinda's deep-brown face was sympathetic. Merrie was such a good-hearted angel, even if she was a little clumsy.

"As you know," said Florinda, "for quite a while, I've been preparing all of you to make your first visits to earth."

"It feels like a million years!" cried Celeste, tossing back her black hair impatiently.

"Celeste, don't exaggerate," scolded Florinda. "It's only been one hundred and fifty years. Rachel needs an angel right away, so I'm going to give you a pop quiz. The angel who gives me the best answer will be sent down to help Rachel. The first question is, What are the largest animals on earth today?"

"Dinosaurs!" said Amber, the smallest of the four angels.

Florinda shook her head. "Amber, you haven't been keeping up with your studies. Dinosaurs disappeared a long time ago. Next question: What is the most beautiful thing on earth?"

"Washing machines!" said Serena, an angel with silky blond hair and an immaculate golden gown. "I love to watch those suds dance around. And I adore the way clothes come out so perfectly!"

"I was thinking of something a little more inspiring," Florinda said.

"Hot fudge sundaes!" Celeste said. "I can't wait to taste one!"

"Not a bad answer, Celeste. Many people—and angels—would agree."

Merrie raised her hand. "I think the most beautiful things on earth are rivers and streams and waterfalls! Especially waterfalls. They make such pretty musical sounds."

Florinda smiled. "Merrie, that's a lovely answer. Very accurate and most creative! You shall be Rachel's guardian angel!"

"Me? Whoopie!" Merrie leaped up from her seat, ready to go. Her long red hair, turquoise gown, and white wings fluttered into an excited blur.

"Patience is still a virtue, Merrie," said Florinda. "Please sit back down and untangle yourself. I need to give you some final instructions. First, remember, on earth you will have many powers that people do not have."

"That's the fun part!" said Merrie, giggling.

"And most people on earth are surprised when they meet an angel. Perhaps you should give Rachel time to get used to you. You might even take a different form for a while. Rachel loves animals, you know . . ."

Merrie nodded, her blue eyes twinkling.

"And Rachel has a lovely singing voice, just like you, Merrie." Indeed, Merrie's voice was famous throughout the heavens. The word *angelic* couldn't begin to describe it.

Florinda stepped forward and wrapped her huge pink wings around Merrie to give her blessing. "Angels," she told the others, "come and give Merrie your blessings, too."

Serena, Celeste, and Amber rushed up to Merrie with such enthusiasm, they all got their wings tangled up. After they sorted out whose wings were whose, Florinda cleared her throat. With great warmth she said, "Merrie, I have total faith in you."

"I promise not to let you down!" Merrie sang out, and shimmering like a shooting star, she flew down to earth.

3

Soaking Wet

When Rachel woke up the next morning, she was smiling. She'd had a wonderful dream: a bird with glittery red wings had flown around her bed singing a cheerful little song. This bird was nothing like the ones she and her dad had seen bird-watching in California. It was out of this world!

"Rachel!" Dr. Summers called from the kitchen. "Hurry and get dressed. You don't want to be late your first day of school."

Under her breath, Rachel whispered, "I'd rather not get there at all!" Her heart began to pound at the thought of being the new girl in class.

But she got out of bed and began rummaging

through her suitcases for something to wear. "Mom! My clothes are all wrinkled!" Rachel shouted.

"The iron is still packed away. I don't remember in which box," answered her mother.

"But I *have* to find it," Rachel insisted. "I can't go to school wrinkled—especially on the first day."

Rachel managed to find the iron, but not the ironing board. So she put a towel on the floor and ironed her blue plaid skirt and a white blouse. Not perfect, but it would have to do.

When Rachel came downstairs, her mother smiled. "You look terrific, Rachel. Breakfast's just cornflakes and milk this morning."

"Mom," Rachel said suddenly, "remember the incredible stories Dad used to tell me about Angel Corners? Do you think there are real angels here?"

Rachel's mother's eyes grew sad. "Your dad loved to tell stories, and he loved growing up here. But he was just teasing you about the angels."

Rachel decided to keep her eye out for angels anyway, just in case.

"I'm a little nervous today, too," admitted Rachel's mother. "This is my first day on the job. Everyone in town loved old Doc Wells so much, it will take me time to earn the town's trust."

"You'll do fine." Rachel smiled at her mother. "You're the smartest person I know!"

"Well, thank you." Dr. Summers smiled back. "That goes double for you."

Suddenly a clap of thunder made mother and daughter jump.

"Uh-oh," Dr. Summers groaned. "If I'm so smart, why can't I remember where we packed the umbrellas?"

They searched through some suitcases and boxes but had no luck.

"It's a good thing your school isn't very far," said Dr. Summers.

Ten minutes later, they arrived at Angel Corners Middle School soaked to the skin.

They dripped all the way to the office, where Dr. Summers enrolled Rachel. Then she gave Rachel a quick hug, said "Good luck!" and was gone.

"Come along," the secretary told Rachel, and she walked her down the hall.

Rachel's stomach did flip-flops as the secretary opened a door and ushered her into a classroom. Instantly, twenty pairs of eyes were staring at her.

"Ms. Fisher, this is Rachel Summers," the secretary announced. "She's just moved to Angel Corners from Los Angeles."

"Welcome." Ms. Fisher smiled warmly. She looked just the way Rachel thought a teacher should look: tall, gray-haired, and sweet. Her glasses made her look extra smart.

Rachel could feel her soggy bangs drooping down her forehead.

A boy in the back row of desks pointed at her and snickered.

"Jimmy Nordstrom, don't be rude!" Ms. Fisher told him. "I'm sure you've been caught in the rain at least once in your life."

The teacher directed Rachel to a seat near the windows. As Rachel sat down, she heard a girl whisper, "What a wet mess."

Everyone's going to think that I always look like this, Rachel told herself.

While Ms. Fisher wrote on the blackboard, Rachel took some notebooks and markers out of her backpack.

After a few minutes she found the courage to begin gazing around the room. A pretty girl with a long blond ponytail and jingly bracelets decided to comb her hair while the teacher's back was turned.

"I hear you, Felicia," Ms. Fisher said. "Your bracelets always give you away."

The whole class laughed and whispered to one another. Rachel smiled a little, too. But nobody whispered to her.

Rachel glanced at the hanging map of the United States, with Hawaii set off alone in a little box. Rachel felt as lonely as Hawaii.

"As you know," said Ms. Fisher, "each year

Rachel, Meet Your Angel!

Angel Corners celebrates Founders Day with a parade and a fair. Mayor Witty has decided that this year, we should raise money to fix the angel clock."

"Great idea!" yelled Jimmy Nordstrom. "I'm sick of hearing it chime seventeen o'clock!"

Rachel remembered the clock she had heard the night before. Her dad had told her stories about the clock in Angel Corners. Every time it chimed, four beautiful angels came dancing out. Rachel sighed. If her father were still alive, she wouldn't be here in this new school, in this new town.

Ms. Fisher continued, "Mayor Witty is asking everyone in town to help. The angel clock is over two hundred years old, and repairing it will be expensive. I want the class to form committees of up to four people. Each committee will need to think of a way to raise money."

A girl with rumpled dark hair raised her hand and waved it around wildly. "Ms. Fisher! Can Val McCall and I be on the same committee?"

"All right, Lulu." Ms. Fisher smiled. "I know you and Val are good friends. I want you to know, though, that I'm saying yes only because the two of you work so well together."

"Yesss!" Lulu cheered and grinned at Val. Rachel couldn't help smiling, too. It was pretty brave of Lulu to ask, Rachel thought.

Before long, everyone in class had formed their

committees. But nobody had chosen Rachel. Ms. Fisher said, "Rachel, I would like you to work with Toby Antonio, Lulu Bliss, and Valentine McCall."

Rachel nodded.

Ms. Fisher continued, "Class, there are many ways you can raise money. You can bake cookies and sell them. Or have a lawn sale of your old toys and books. Or have an auction or raffle. Use your imagination!"

Then it was time for geography. Ms. Fisher's class was studying Mexico, which Rachel had already studied in Los Angeles. That was a relief.

For the rest of the morning, nobody paid the slightest attention to her.

4

First Lunch

W hen the lunch bell rang, everyone dashed out the door. Rachel stood up, not having any idea where the lunchroom was.

"Follow me," said Ms. Fisher briskly. "I'll show you where to go."

At the end of the hall, Ms. Fisher pointed to the noisy cafeteria, then walked away.

Rachel wasn't the least bit hungry, but she bought some spaghetti and chocolate milk. Then she began searching for a place to sit down.

At one table, Rachel recognized the ponytailed blond girl who'd been combing her hair in class. The seat next to her was empty, so Rachel walked over and began to sit down.

"This seat is taken," the girl hissed angrily. She tossed her hair and clinked her bracelets, reminding Rachel of a startled rattlesnake.

"Oh, I'm sorry," Rachel apologized, and she began backing away.

"Here's a seat," called a cheerful voice near a window.

"Thanks," Rachel said, gratefully hurrying over.

"Hi," said the girl with a smile. She had warm green eyes and freckles and her hair was in a braid that almost reached her waist. "I'm Toby Antonio. We're on the same Founders Day committee."

"Right. Hi." Rachel smiled shyly and sat down.

"Mayor Witty came into our bakery yesterday. He told us you'd moved in. Your mom's the new vet, right?"

"Gosh." Rachel shook her head. "This *is* a small town! In Los Angeles nobody knows anything about *anyone.*"

"I'm wild about animals," Toby said.

"Me, too." Rachel smiled at her. She noticed that Toby was wearing tights with pink leg warmers over them. "Are you a dancer?" Rachel asked.

"Mmmm—yes—at least I'm *trying* to be," Toby said with her mouth full. "I take a lot of lessons."

Then they couldn't think of anything else to say. Suddenly, Rachel blurted out. "Toby, are there angels in Angel Corners? My dad used to tell me . . ."

Rachel, Meet Your Angel!

Toby made a face. "Nope! The town is named after a waterfall, that's all."

They were quiet again, and then Toby said, "Los Angeles sounds so glamorous! Now, *that's* the City of Angels! Have you ever gone to the ballet or to a Lakers game?"

"Yes, both!" Rachel grinned. "My dad and I used to play basketball sometimes in our driveway. But I think I'm too short to really play."

"No, you're not!" Toby shook her head so fiercely her braid bounced from side to side. "Some of the best players in the NBA are short. We ought to shoot baskets together sometime."

"Really?" Rachel asked eagerly.

"Mm-hmm." Toby twirled her spaghetti around her fork.

Rachel was beginning to feel better. She looked around the lunchroom and noticed that the seat next to the pretty blond girl was still empty.

"Who is that girl with the bracelets?" Rachel whispered to Toby.

Toby rolled her eyes. "That's Felicia McWithers. Her family has lived in Angel Corners for generations. Felicia thinks that makes her important. I think she's a pain!"

"Do you know her very well?" Rachel asked.

"*Too* well." Toby made a face. "I've known Felicia since nursery school. She's always been

17

bossy. And she has to have everything her own way. I tried to be her friend once, but it didn't work. Felicia has never forgiven me."

As Toby spoke, she waved over two girls. "Val! Lulu! Come and sit with us."

Rachel recognized the girls as the two others who were on her Founders Day committee.

"Hi," Val said, smiling at Rachel shyly. Val was stunning. She had curly copper hair and amazing violet eyes. She was wearing black leggings under an oversized red plaid shirt, and she wore a baseball cap backward. Val's sneakers were the same plaid as her shirt.

"Val is the most glamorous girl in the fifth grade," Toby announced.

"Toby!" Val blushed.

"Felicia McWithers works her butt off to be glamorous," Toby continued, "but Val does it without even trying."

"I don't usually look this awful," Rachel explained. "We got caught in the rain."

Lulu grinned. "Just like Gene Kelly in that famous dance in *Singin' in the Rain.*" Lulu leaped up and began singing and dancing.

Val rolled her eyes. "Lulu's wild about movies."

"Hey, Rachel," said Lulu, sitting down again, "I wish I had the rain as an excuse for *my* clothes. My dad says I look like an unmade bed."

Val flung her arm around Lulu and declared, "Lulu Bliss is my best friend in the world, and she can look any old way she likes! Did you notice her socks, Rachel?"

One of Lulu's socks was green and one blue.

"Matching socks are totally boring," Lulu insisted.

Rachel noticed that Lulu and Val were wearing matching friendship bracelets, however. For a minute she thought about all her old friends in Los Angeles.

She came back to the here and now when she heard Toby ask, "When should we have our first committee meeting?"

"Tomorrow is Saturday," said Lulu. "Let's have the meeting in the morning—at Toby's house."

Toby grinned. "You just love the free doughnuts Mom and Dad give us, Lulu."

"Correct!" Lulu nodded.

"Uh-oh, there's the bell," Val announced. They all headed back to class. As they walked down the hall, Rachel heard some jingling behind her.

It was Felicia. She glared at Toby.

"I wouldn't make friends with this new person," she said huffily. "She looks like something the cat dragged in."

Toby's green eyes flared. "Thanks for the advice, Felicia, but you're a fine one to give advice about friendship!"

"Have fun with your little committee," Felicia said with a sneer, hurrying off.

Rachel's spirits sank again as she walked back into class. *There's something frightening about that Felicia,* she thought.

5

A Sweet Dream

After school, Toby reminded Rachel about their committee meeting. "See you tomorrow at my house, at ten o'clock sharp. Remember, don't eat breakfast. My family owns a bakery."

"I'll be there," Rachel promised. She could hardly wait.

As Rachel walked home, she noticed how small and cozy the houses were in Angel Corners. Most had front porches with swings and hummingbird feeders in the yard. She saw weathervanes with golden angels on them, too.

When Rachel reached her own little gray house, she found her mother outside, checking to see if there was any mail in the mailbox.

"So how did your first day go?" she asked Rachel.

"Pretty good. I'm on a committee already. And I met some really nice girls."

"Great!" Dr. Summers looked relieved. "Your dad always said that Angel Corners was a friendly town. I've had a pretty good day, too, Rachel. Come and meet my first patient."

Dr. Summers's office was in the back of the house, with a separate entrance. She unlocked the door and led Rachel inside. There she opened a big cage and lifted out a Siberian husky puppy.

"Ooh!" Rachel crooned. She could never resist puppies.

"He belongs to Mayor Witty," explained Dr. Summers. "He found him at the town dump. Can you imagine? The poor pup is in terrible shape."

Rachel could see that his blue eyes were cloudy, and his fur thin and dull. The pup was so skinny she could see his ribs.

"Poor guy!" Rachel couldn't bear to see animals suffer. She cried enough to need three tissues each time she watched a *Lassie* rerun. "What's his name?" she asked.

"The mayor named him Hercules, after an ancient Greek hero. Little pup, I hope you have the strength of Hercules! You are going to need it to get better!"

Later, as Dr. Summers tended to the puppy, Rachel finished unpacking. She ironed the rest of her clothes, so she'd look a lot more presentable in school on Monday.

That night, Rachel dreamed of the little red bird again. This time, the bird did not sing like a bird but like a terrific soprano—like Whitney Houston! And she was flying around Rachel and Hercules.

In the morning, for the first time since her father had died, Rachel herself really *felt* like singing. She jumped out of bed and dressed quickly.

"No breakfast for me," Rachel told her mom. "I'm eating at Toby's. How's Hercules today?"

"Not so good." Dr. Summers frowned. "He doesn't seem to be responding to the antibiotics. I feel pretty helpless."

She poured another cup of coffee and gazed out at the sunny day. "Rachel, why don't we take a walk in the woods before you go to your meeting?"

"No, thanks." Rachel shuddered. "The woods are spooky. I'll stick to the sidewalk."

"Another time," said her mother. "Your dad loved those woods when he was a boy. He told me he carved his initials on one of the trees."

"I'll look for them . . . some other day," Rachel said. Then she dashed out the door and ran to Antonios' Bakery, just down the block.

Toby was behind the counter wearing a white

baker's apron over her jeans and striped T-shirt. Her long braid was all pinned up. She was carefully putting a blueberry pie into a box.

A woman who looked exactly like Toby, only twenty years older, was helping a boy select a dozen different doughnuts. Toby's dad, who was tall and had frizzy red hair, was ringing up a sale.

"Rachel, this is my mom and dad," Toby said.

"I heard about your father," Mr. Antonio said sympathetically. "I'm really sorry. I knew him when we were boys. We used to race each other to Angel Falls, and he always beat me! Boy, was he fast!"

"Really?" Rachel smiled. It cheered her to think of her dad as a boy in Angel Corners.

"I'll be back in a second," Toby said. She went into the kitchen and returned with a huge tray of doughnuts, some iced cinnamon buns, and four tall glasses of milk.

"Can you eat all the doughnuts you want?" asked Rachel, eagerly eyeing the goodies.

Toby nodded. "Sure. But I'd better not—unless I want to dance like one of the hippopotamuses in that Disney cartoon. What's the name of it?"

"*Fantasia!*" Lulu yelled, coming into the bakery with Val. "It's one of the Disney studio's best animated features—"

"Okay, okay!" Toby held up her hand. "Stop!"

Today Lulu was wearing a blue polka-dot shirt

24

and striped green jeans. The colors clashed so badly, they almost hurt Rachel's eyes.

"Cool camera," Rachel said.

"Dad gave it to me for my birthday," Lulu said proudly. "I take it everywhere." She aimed her camera at Rachel.

Click! The flash went off, leaving Rachel seeing red dots in front of her.

"Ms. Fisher made Lulu stop bringing her camera to school," Val told Rachel. "She said it drove her bonkers."

Through the red dots, Rachel noticed that Val's sneakers matched her mint-green overalls.

"Val, do you have matching sneakers for every outfit?" Rachel couldn't resist asking.

"Yes." Lulu answered for her. "You see, Val's mom owns a travel agency, and she travels a lot. Each time she leaves Val, she feels guilty. So she brings her new clothes—with sneakers to match."

"Mom's great," Val said. "I love the sneakers, but I wish she wouldn't travel so much."

Toby picked up the tray of goodies. "Follow me," she told the others. "Let's have our meeting in the attic."

"Cool!" Lulu cheered. "It's like being in another world up there."

The girls walked through the side door in the bakery kitchen and entered the house.

"Ignore the messy bedrooms," Toby called back over her shoulder as they walked upstairs. "They belong to my disgusting brothers."

"I always thought brothers might be nice," Rachel said. "Sometimes being an only child gets lonely."

"I'll trade you anytime," Toby teased.

Rachel's eyes went wide when she saw the attic. It was a truly magical room!

6

A Little Red Bird Told Me

Rachel felt like she'd walked into the second act of *Swan Lake*. One whole wall of the room was a mural of ballerinas dancing in swan costumes under a silver moon. They looked as if they might dance off the wall at any moment.

"My grandmother was a famous dancer," Toby explained. "She used to practice in this room when she was a girl."

"It's dreamy." Rachel beamed.

One wall had a big mirror and a ballet barre. A grand piano stood in a corner.

The morning sun poured into the room through wide windows. "If I lived here, I'd never leave this room!" Rachel declared.

Then she noticed a miniature basketball hoop in another corner.

"I couldn't resist putting it up!" Toby grinned. "I just can't choose between basketball and ballet."

"Then don't," Rachel answered.

The four girls tugged some overstuffed chairs into the middle of the room and used an old trunk as a table.

"Okay," Toby said after they were all settled. "Since this is my house, I'll call the first meeting to order. Um, does anyone have any ideas on raising money to fix the angel clock?"

Lulu, Val, and Rachel shook their heads.

For a while, the only sounds were of cinnamon buns and doughnuts being eaten and blue jays squawking outside.

Suddenly Val perked up. "I have an idea! Let's have a fashion show. We could use my clothes. I've got a closet full—"

"You just want to show off for Zeb Burgess," Lulu teased.

"No, I don't," Val insisted. "Zeb Burgess would never be caught dead at a fashion show."

"Nobody will pay money to see your clothes when they can see them for free any day," said Lulu. She bit into a jelly doughnut, getting a smudge of powdered sugar on her nose.

"How about this," said Toby. "Why don't we

have a dance benefit? I'll do my solo as the Sugar Plum Fairy."

Val shook her head. "A dance is too complicated! You have to rehearse and find a stage . . ."

"That's true," said Toby sadly. She turned to Rachel. "Do you have any ideas?"

As Rachel was about to say no, she happened to look out the window. A small red bird—just like the one in her dreams—was perched on the window ledge. And behind it, over the treetops, Rachel saw a huge orange hot-air balloon.

"Hey, look!" Rachel pointed.

"Oh, that's my mother's," said Val casually. "At least, she rents it sometimes and hangs a sign on it to advertise her travel agency."

Rachel leaped up from her chair. "I just got a great idea! Let's sell raffle tickets and make the prize a ride in the balloon."

"Way to go!" Val beamed. "Why didn't *I* think of that? I'm sure Mom would help us arrange it."

"All in favor say aye," Toby said.

"Aye!" they all shouted together.

"Any other official business?" asked Toby.

Lulu's hand shot up. "I think our committee needs a name."

There was general agreement.

"Okay, let's all try to think of one," suggested Toby.

The room got quiet again.

Then Rachel piped up. "Since we're raising money to fix the angel clock, why don't we call ourselves the Angel Club?"

"Great!" Lulu whooped.

"Very elegant," Val crooned.

"OK! It's official," announced Toby. "From now on, we're calling ourselves the Angel Club!"

"Yaay!" They all gave each other high-fives.

"I've got to snap a picture of this historic moment," Lulu said.

She set the timer on her camera. Then she ran back and sat with Rachel, Lulu, and Val—the founding members of the Angel Club!

Click! The photo was taken—the one that would soon be hanging in each member's bedroom.

Meanwhile, quite a distance away, another angel club was meeting.

Florinda and her angels-in-training were watching the girls on earth while eating lunch in the Celestial Cafeteria.

"Florinda," Serena wondered, "can Rachel and her friends do that? I thought *we* were the only angel club."

"The earth needs as many angel clubs as it can get," insisted Florinda. "There are so many problems down there."

Rachel, Meet Your Angel!

Celeste was happily nibbling on her ambrosia and sipping her nectar. "You can always count on cafeteria food," she said confidently.

"When you visit earth," Florinda said, "you may find their cafeteria food less wonderful."

Serena gazed down at Rachel with her newfound friends. "I haven't seen any sign of Merrie yet. Rachel's been doing all the work. Why isn't Merrie helping?"

"Why, Merrie's been helping all along!" said Florinda, surprised.

Amber nodded. "I know what form she's taken!"

"Well, don't tell the others," Florinda said to her. "Serena and Celeste, please keep on watching! You obviously need a lot more training—or else glasses!"

The angels flushed bright red and turned their attention back to earth.

They saw Val licking powdered sugar off her fingers and heard her ask, "What should we charge for the raffle tickets?"

"First let's find out what it costs to rent the balloon," said Toby. "Then we'll decide."

Rachel grinned at Toby. "You're so practical!"

"Tell that to my mom and dad," Toby said, rolling her eyes.

"Let's go ask my mother about the balloon ride," said Val. "The travel agency is still open."

"Okay," agreed Toby. "I hereby declare the first meeting of the Angel Club adjourned."

"Great meeting," Rachel said.

"Rachel, you were great!" Toby flung her arm around her. "You thought up the balloon ride *and* our name."

"I guess I did," said Rachel, pleased with herself. Then she remembered the little red bird and marveled at how many red birds she'd seen since moving to Angel Corners.

As they left the bakery, Toby tapped Rachel's shoulder. "I'll race you to the end of the block."

"You got it!" Rachel ran off as fast as she could.

It was no contest. Toby took such big strides, she easily reached the corner first.

But Rachel didn't mind at all. It felt so great to be Toby's friend—and a member of the Angel Club!

7

The Angel Clock Strikes Again

Toby and Rachel waited on the corner for Lulu and Val to catch up.

Toby picked a sprig of periwinkle and stuck it in her hair. "These grow everywhere in the woods."

"Do you really go in there?" Rachel asked admiringly. "That place gives me the creeps!"

"I guess I've never thought about it, since I just grew up with them. It's great in there!" Toby insisted. "Sometimes I practice my ballet near Angel Falls. It's like dancing in a fairy tale."

Val and Lulu were taking a long time to catch up. They walked along slowly, chattering away. *I wish I had a friend like that,* Rachel thought to herself. *I wonder if Toby has a best friend.*

"Uh-oh!" Toby groaned, pointing. "Here comes Felicia and her little slave, Andrea."

Felicia was striding toward them like a general leading an army. But Felicia's army was just one small, pale girl with a sad, mousy face.

"Hi, there!" Felicia said, smirking. "If you're trying to find the *best* way to raise money for Founders Day, you may as well save your brain cells. *My* committee"—she pointed at Andrea—"has great plans."

"Really?" said Toby calmly. "What are they?"

Felicia waited for Lulu and Val to join her audience. Then she announced, "*I'm* going to sell tickets for a tour of my house. We have fabulous antiques! People will happily pay ten dollars a ticket to see them."

"That's a lot of money," commented Rachel.

Felicia glared at her. "You're just jealous because *I'm* going to make more money than you. Wait and see. I'm going to make more money than *anyone*!"

Rachel backed away. Felicia was so fierce!

Lulu whispered to Rachel, "Felicia reminds me of the monstrous child that Patty Duke played in *The Bad Seed*."

"I heard that," Felicia snapped. Then she turned to Toby and said, "What are *you* planning to do? If you are desperate, I might consider letting you join *my* committee."

"No, thanks," Toby told her. "And our project is

a secret. Let's go," she told the Angel Club, and they hurried away.

On Main Street, Lulu stopped at a newsstand. "I have to pick up *Premiere* magazine for my dad."

The owner of the newsstand was a tall, handsome, young black man. He wore railroad overalls and a baseball cap.

"This is Derek Weatherby," Lulu told Rachel. "He knows everything there is to know about Angel Corners."

Derek laughed. "Lulu, you just flatter me because I let you look at the magazines for free." He turned to Rachel. "And what do you say your name is?"

"I'm Rachel Summers. I just moved here from Los Angeles."

"Los Angeles?" said Derek. "I used to live there! But then I found this little piece of heaven."

"I thought you *always* lived here," said Lulu, amazed. "How do you know so much about Angel Corners?"

"Well, Lulu, I get around. I use my eyes, my ears, and my bike—and I'm at the library every chance I get. I think I've read every back issue of the *Angel Corners Gazette.*"

"My stepfather is the publisher," Val chimed in.

Derek handed Rachel a copy of the newspaper. "Consider it a welcome-to-Angel-Corners present!"

"Thank you, Mr. Weatherby," Rachel said politely.

"Puh-leeze!" Derek made a face. "Call me Derek!"

"I will," Rachel promised. She felt instantly there was something special about Derek. Rachel couldn't put it into words, but she felt it in her bones.

It was almost noon, and the angel clock was about to chime.

"Let's watch it," suggested Rachel. "If I'm going to raise money to fix this clock, I want to know what it looks like!"

Bing! The clock began chiming. A blue door opened, and out danced four once-gilded angels twirling around in a graceful circle.

Bing! Bing! Bing! The clock chimed on, all the way to seventeen.

Rachel giggled.

"Let's go!" urged Val. "Mom's closing in half an hour."

They all rushed over to the travel agency. Val's mother was as elegant as her daughter. She looked a little like Val, but her hair was even redder, shinier, and shorter.

Val's stepsister, Tracy, was there, too. "This is my little blister!" Val joked.

"Your what?" asked Rachel as Tracy poked Val and began to wrestle with her.

"She's the little pain that is always on my heels!" Val said.

They all laughed, but Rachel could see that Tracy and Val liked each other.

The Angel Club explained their raffle project to Val's mother. She flipped open a leather appointment book. "You're in luck, girls. I have the balloon reserved for one hour on Founders Day. I'll donate it to your committee. Then all the raffle money can go toward fixing the clock."

"Thank you!" said the Angel Club together.

"Uh-oh." Lulu rolled her eyes. "Look who's peeking in the window."

"It's Felicia." Val waved merrily at her.

Felicia stuck out her tongue, then ran away.

"She's spying on us, trying to find out our project," said Toby.

"But I don't understand why," said Rachel.

"Because Felicia always has to know everything!" Toby explained. "She thinks if she does, then she can find out a way to win. She can't stand it if somebody else does. It runs in her family."

"Girls," said Ms. McCall, "did you know there's a flea market on Main Street tomorrow? You could sell a lot of tickets there."

"Great idea!" Lulu said. "I can use the photocopier at my dad's store to print up the tickets tonight."

"Okay," said Toby. "Let's meet under the angel clock tomorrow at noon."

On her way home, Rachel passed the angel clock again. Wouldn't it be great if there really *were* angels?

When Rachel passed the newsstand, Derek called out, "Don't be a stranger."

"I won't," she called back. As she walked along, she kept her eyes on the sky, hoping that tiny red bird would appear again.

Could it be just a coincidence that the bird looked exactly like the one in her dreams?

Soon, Rachel gave up looking for it. She began worrying about selling raffle tickets instead. She felt like regular old shy Rachel again. *I don't know anyone here except the members of the Angel Club,* she thought. *How can I just walk up to strangers and ask them to buy tickets?*

She worried about it the rest of the way home.

8

The Wonderful, Terrible Flea Market

The next morning Rachel woke up early. While she was brushing her teeth, she thought she saw something red and shimmery in the mirror. But as quickly as she saw it, it was gone!

She headed downstairs first to her mother's office to see how the mayor's puppy was doing. Little Hercules was lying in the corner of his cage, looking even more pathetic than yesterday. His eyes were completely closed.

"Poor Hercules," Rachel said sadly. "You could use a guardian angel."

"Mayor Witty keeps calling up to check on him. He says that if I can save Hercules, I'll be the best vet he ever met!" said Rachel's mother.

"You're *already* the best vet!" Rachel insisted. She pressed her face against the bars of the cage. "Hercules, we love you! Please get well, okay?"

Hercules weakly opened his eyes. But he quickly closed them again.

Rachel sighed as she got up to go.

She ran all the way to Main Street, waving to Derek as she passed his newsstand.

"I love flea markets," he called out. "Everyone buys my 'antique' magazines."

The tables were already set up around the village green. Lots of eager buyers milled around, eyeing the bargains.

Rachel and Toby reached the angel clock at the same time.

"Lulu and Val had a sleepover together last night," Toby said. "I bet they overslept!"

"We did not!" Val and Lulu had sneaked up behind them. "But we stayed up late," said Val, "because Lulu wanted to watch every angel movie ever made."

"Right!" Lulu laughed. *"Angels with Dirty Faces, The Trouble with Angels, Angels in the Outfield—"*

Toby put her hand over Lulu's mouth. "We get it!" she said.

"Do you think there really are angels?" Rachel asked Lulu.

"Yes!" Lulu nodded.

"Oh, you believe in the tooth fairy, too," Toby said teasingly.

Today, Lulu wore bright red overalls with a purple blouse. Her hair was messy, as usual, and she was holding a huge hatbox.

Val, looking hip in baggy pants and an extra-large sweatshirt, was holding a hatbox, too. "Lulu and I stayed up late making special hats for the Angel Club so that people would notice us selling tickets," Val explained.

"Ta-da!" sang Lulu, opening her box and lifting out a wide-brimmed straw hat. Two pink satin angel's wings stuck out jauntily from either side of the crown.

"You two are geniuses!" Toby smiled. She plunked a hat on her head. So did Lulu and Val.

Rachel felt silly as she put hers on. She wasn't so sure she wanted to be so conspicuous.

"Here are the raffle tickets." Val handed each girl a bunch. "Why don't we break up into teams? Lulu and I will take this side of the green."

Toby nudged her with an elbow. "You want this side because Zeb Burgess is here, selling T-shirts for the swim team." Toby turned to Rachel. "Are you boy-crazy, too?" she asked.

"Not very much." Rachel shrugged.

"I am, a little," confessed Toby. "But it's mostly for basketball players. Hey, look!" Toby grabbed

Rachel's hand. "There's a big crowd around the comic book booth. Let's go get 'em."

Toby began waving the tickets around, shouting, "Raffle tickets! Get your raffle tickets! For just one dollar, you can win a ride in a balloon."

"Really?" asked an eager woman. "What kind of balloon?"

"The huge orange one! You know, like the balloon from that movie *Around the World in Eighty Days.*"

"I'll take one." The lady handed Toby a dollar.

"See?" Toby poked Rachel. "Selling these tickets is a cinch!"

Rachel nodded, but she felt shy. There was no way she could yell and jump around like Toby.

A skinny man frying funnel cakes handed Toby a dollar. Then she walked up to the man who sold wind-up toys, and he bought five tickets!

"Toby, you're incredible!" Rachel exclaimed. "I wish I could do that."

"It's easy as pie!" Toby grinned.

In just forty-five minutes, Toby sold twenty raffle tickets.

"Now it's your turn," she told Rachel. "I need a break. Actually, what I really need is a bathroom."

Toby tossed Rachel her tiny drawstring purse that held the money and raffle tickets. "Hold this for me. I'll be back in a flash."

Rachel, Meet Your Angel!

"I'll meet you under the clock," Rachel said. As soon as Toby left, a lady with a poodle on a leash came walking toward Rachel. "Ex-excuse me," Rachel began, but she spoke so softly, the lady passed her right by.

Rachel saw Felicia's friend Andrea walking up to her. At least she was a familiar face.

"Hi," said Andrea in her wispy voice. "Can I buy a ticket? I'd love to win a ride."

"Sure!" Rachel smiled gratefully. "You're my first customer."

But just as Andrea was about to hand Rachel a dollar, they both saw Felicia coming toward them.

"Never mind!" muttered Andrea. She stuck the dollar back in her pocket.

Poor Andrea, thought Rachel. *She doesn't take a breath unless Felicia approves. I wonder why.*

Rachel halfheartedly tried selling some more tickets. She practiced the words in her head, but when people walked by, she was too shy to say them. "I give up," she said, defeated. "I'll wait for Toby to come back."

Suddenly, Rachel remembered that her mother's birthday was tomorrow. The flea market would be a great place to find a present. Rachel had saved twenty dollars of her allowance for it.

Rachel saw a woman from the chamber of commerce selling miniature china versions of the angel

43

clock. That was the perfect gift! *Mom will love it,* Rachel thought.

The clock cost exactly nineteen dollars. The woman wrapped it in tissue paper and put it in a shopping bag.

Then Rachel felt thirsty. A cup of lemonade cost a dollar, exactly the amount she had left.

She noticed that the lemonade stand was next to a folding table where Felicia was sitting. Andrea stood next to her holding a sign that said, TOUR THE MOST BEAUTIFUL HOUSE IN ANGEL CORNERS FOR ONLY $10!

A fancy china bowl that was meant to hold the ticket money was empty. Ten dollars a ticket was just too much.

It was one o'clock, and the angel clock began to chime. Rachel flopped down on the grass and put the shopping bag and Toby's purse beside her.

Bing! Bing! The clock struck, and the angels danced out. Rachel watched until they did their last graceful twirls.

Rachel imagined sitting there watching that clock all day! But then she felt guilty. She was letting the Angel Club down. *I have to try harder to sell these raffle tickets,* she thought.

Rachel reached over for her shopping bag and Toby's purse. Rachel gulped. The shopping bag was there—but Toby's purse was gone!

9

Catastrophe!

R achel felt a wave of panic flow over her. She called out to the woman selling the clocks. "Did you see anyone take my purse?"

"Sorry, dear, I didn't." The woman shook her head.

Rachel looked all around. There was no trace of Toby's purse.

But here was Toby running toward her, with her long braid flying.

"Sorry I took so long to get back," she apologized. "The closest bathroom was at home."

Rachel nodded, her heart beating like crazy.

"So," Toby said, smiling, "how many tickets have you sold?"

"Uh, none . . ." Rachel began.

Toby said, "I guess you need more lessons from me. Give me my purse, and let's go."

"Toby"—Rachel gulped—"I have to tell you something—"

"What?" Toby asked impatiently.

"Something terrible has happened! You see, I put your purse down for a few seconds while I watched the clock chime . . . and when I went to pick it up again, your purse was gone!"

"What?" Toby's eyes widened. "Rachel, are you telling me that you lost all the money?" Now she was glaring. "You lost all twenty dollars?"

"Yes." Rachel looked down at the ground. Her voice trembled. "Oh, Toby, I'm so sorry! You worked hard to sell those tickets."

"I certainly did!" Toby scowled.

"I'm sorry," Rachel repeated. "I don't know what to say—"

"Oh, Rachel," sang out Felicia from her table, "why don't you show Toby the pretty little clock you just bought?"

"What?" said Rachel, perplexed.

"*You* know," smirked Felicia. "The clock in your shopping bag. The one that I saw you buy for nineteen dollars."

Rachel began explaining to Toby. "It's a birthday present for my mother. I bought it with my allowance money."

"Rachel, *really*," said Felicia, "you *know* that's not true! I saw you take Toby's money out of her purse."

"What?" Rachel was so astonished that her mouth fell open.

"Toby," continued Felicia in her snakelike voice, "I saw her take that money out *with my very own two eyes.*"

"I saw her, too!" Andrea piped up.

"That's not true!" said Rachel helplessly. She couldn't believe Felicia was doing this horrible thing. Toby would never be her friend now!

"All I know," said Toby, "is that you were in charge of the Angel Club money, Rachel! And now it's all gone!" Toby glared at her again, then turned and ran away.

"Toby, stop!" Rachel shouted. "Oh, please stop!"

But she didn't try to run after her. Rachel was so stunned, she didn't know what to do.

Felicia grinned at Rachel maliciously. Rachel stared back, wanting to pull Felicia's ponytail right out of her head!

Andrea looked away.

At least she's a little ashamed, Rachel thought.

Finally, Rachel just turned around and ran home. At least she wouldn't give Felicia the satisfaction of seeing her cry.

10

The Star Chamber

But Florinda and her angels-in-training *did* see Rachel cry. They were in the Star Chamber at that moment, studying Advanced Dreamology.

"Florinda," Amber asked, "can't Merrie stop that horrible Felicia from lying about Rachel? She's doing so much harm—and just when Rachel and Toby were getting to be friends!"

Florinda sighed. "This is one of the hardest lessons we angels need to learn. Sometimes, we cannot prevent bad things from happening. If we could, it would be like controlling life. Nobody can do that—not even us!"

Celeste nodded and wrote in her golden notebook, "LIFE ON EARTH IS COMPLICATED."

"But what *can* we do?" asked Serena eagerly.

"Oh, we can do so much," said Florinda. "We can give people dreams to hold on to!"

The Queen of the Angels aimed her crystal pointer at the walls of the Star Chamber, which sparkled with murals depicting popular dreams. There were "Perfect Love," and "Buckets of Dollars," and "Getting a New Car for Graduation."

"Angels," instructed Florinda, "these are some of the most common dreams on earth. But there are many wonderful dreams that we can give people! Dreams as countless as the stars. Dreams that bring hope and confidence! People simply cannot live without these dreams."

"Can I really *give* people happy dreams?" Amber asked.

"You bright angel!" Florinda beamed at her. "Yes, you can! In fact, you can give your particular child any dream you like."

Florinda gazed down at Rachel, her eyes bright with hope. "If Merrie hasn't been sleeping through all her dream lessons, she could help Rachel right now with a strong dream to hold on to. Oh, I hope she remembers what I've taught her."

The angels-in-training directed their attention back to Angel Corners. They saw Rachel run into her house, dash up the stairs, and throw herself onto her bed.

"Toby hates me now," Rachel sobbed. "And I don't blame her. And when she tells Lulu and Val, they'll hate me, too. I wanted so much to be in the Angel Club."

Rachel tried to think of a way she could pay Toby back the money. But she had spent her last penny at the flea market.

Rachel cried until she was so exhausted, she fell asleep.

And that's when she dreamed that an angel came and sat on her bed! As the angel spoke reassuringly, she gently brushed Rachel's damp hair away from her face. It felt heavenly! "Rachel, remember how your dad used to say that you could do anything you set your mind to? Try to remember that. And think about all the happy times that you and he shared. Surely, those memories will help you, too."

Rachel woke up in excellent spirits. Something magical was definitely happening.

Suddenly she felt hungry. She found her mother in the kitchen, feeding Hercules.

"Hi, pup!" Rachel crooned. "Are you feeling any better?"

"He's still a sick little guy," said Dr. Summers with a sigh. She finished feeding the puppy and put him into his cage. Then she said, "Rachel, I'm too bushed to cook tonight. How about ordering a pizza from Angelo's?"

"Doesn't *angelo* mean "angel" in Italian?" Rachel asked.

"Yes." Her mother nodded.

"Angels seem to be all around us in this town," Rachel said softly, remembering her dream. "Hey, Mom, I know it's not your birthday until tomorrow, but can I give you your present now? Even if it's not wrapped?"

"Sure!" said her mother.

Rachel raced into her bedroom and rushed back with the gift.

"Oh, my!" Dr. Summers gasped when she saw the china clock. "It's lovely, Rachel. I'll treasure it forever." She leaned over and gave Rachel a kiss.

"I'll put it in a place of honor, right on the mantel," said Dr. Summers. "Now, let's figure out what kind of pizza we should get."

"Anything without mushrooms," Rachel said quickly.

"You got it."

All through dinner that night, Rachel couldn't stop thinking about Toby. *If I call her, I bet she'll hang up on me. What can I do? I don't have the money to give back to her. How can I convince Toby that I didn't steal it?*

"Earth to Rachel," said her mother gently. "Something has been bothering you since you came home today. Do you want to tell me about it?"

"Yes," Rachel said gratefully. Then she poured out the whole story, including Felicia's lie. "I should never have put down that purse! I'm so mad at myself!"

"How much money did you lose?" asked her mother.

"Twenty dollars. Every cent of it earned by Toby." Rachel felt near tears again.

Dr. Summers gazed at her daughter sympathetically. "Suppose I lend you the twenty dollars to repay Toby."

"Would you?" Rachel asked eagerly.

"Yes, but you'll have to earn it back. I have the perfect job for you."

"I'll do *anything*!" Rachel promised.

"I want you to take care of Hercules," said her mother. "He needs more attention than I can give him now."

"Taking care of Hercules isn't a job," Rachel said brightly. "It's fun."

"It *is* a job," insisted Dr. Summers, "and a tremendous responsibility. He's a very sick puppy."

"I'll take great care of him," Rachel promised.

Rachel spent the rest of the evening with Hercules, first feeding him and then holding him gently and singing softly, because TLC is also important for getting well.

Rachel, Meet Your Angel!

While Hercules napped, Rachel thought about what the angel had said in her dream that afternoon. *She says I'll feel better if I remember the happy times I had with Dad.* Rachel thought about how she and her dad had always given each other spectacular, handmade birthday cards.

That gave Rachel a great idea. She got out her pastel crayons and watercolors and began to create a colorful card for Toby. Tomorrow, she would give her the card with the money.

Rachel drew all the angel-y things she could think of: the angel clock, the Angel Club meeting in Toby's attic, her dream angel, and even Hercules with a guardian angel watching over him.

Then she added Toby wearing ballet slippers and her Angel Club hat with its pink satin wings. She wrote:

Dear Toby,
    You are such an angel!
    I would never *ever* want to hurt you!
    Please believe me! I did not take a penny!
    I borrowed this money from my mother to pay you back for the twenty dollars I lost.
    And I am going to sell lots of raffle tickets! Just you wait and see!

                                    Love,
                                    Rachel

"Toby's got to believe that I didn't steal her money!" Rachel said fiercely.

But even if Toby did believe her, Rachel had another problem: How was she going to find the courage to sell her share of the raffle tickets?

"Hercules," she said out loud, "we've got to be strong. We've *got* to!"

11

(Un)Heavenly Choir

On Monday, Rachel got up early to feed Hercules. Then she hurried to school so she could get there before everyone else. She raced into the classroom and slipped the card and money inside Toby's desk.

Then she sat down and stuck her nose into a book, waiting for the bell to ring.

Rachel's heart pounded when Toby came walking in. She watched her as she raised the top of her desk.

Rachel saw Toby's green eyes grow wide as she discovered the surprise.

As soon as Toby finished reading the card, she turned to Rachel with a huge smile.

"Thank you!" Toby mouthed silently.

"You're very welcome," Rachel whispered. She was so relieved that their fight was over. She and Toby were friends again!

Felicia was watching this whole scene, Rachel noticed. Well, let her! She'd never come between Rachel and Toby again.

Ms. Fisher began the class by asking how all the Founders Day projects were going.

Toby proudly announced, "Our committee has sold sixty dollars' worth of raffle tickets. And we've only just begun."

"Right!" cheered Val and Lulu.

"Good work!" Ms. Fisher congratulated the Angel Club members.

Jimmy Nordstrom and his committee told how they'd sold their duplicate baseball cards.

"Now, that's imaginative recycling!" Ms. Fisher beamed.

Felicia's face was totally grim. Neither she nor Andrea had raised her hand to report on their committee. With some satisfaction, Rachel told herself that they probably hadn't sold any tickets yet. But then, neither had she.

When it was time for everyone to go to Mr. Murphy's room for music class, Rachel rushed over to Toby. "Please believe me!" Rachel said urgently. "I didn't take your—"

Toby interrupted. "It's okay, Rachel. I know you didn't take the money. Felicia has pulled so many sneaky tricks, I wouldn't be a bit surprised if she was the real thief."

Rachel nodded. "But if that's true, how will we be able to prove it?"

When the class reached Mr. Murphy's room, he was already seated at the piano. "As you know," he boomed in his deep bass voice, "every Founders Day, the entire town sings the official Angel Corners anthem together. We haven't sung it since *last* Founders Day, so we had better run through it a few times now."

"Do we have to?" said a few boys.

"Yes, we have to." Mr. Murphy glared. "And I think you should sing standing up, so you can give it some oomph."

"Lots of oomph coming up," said Toby impishly. From the first note, she sang louder than anyone else in class and totally off-key.

Rachel admired Toby's enthusiasm. She didn't give a hoot if she didn't sing perfectly.

Since Rachel didn't know the Angel Corners song, she just stood there, listening. The tune was cheerful and the lyrics were corny, all about hopes taking wing and bright hearts singing. Rachel liked it. It reminded her of the angel in her dream—and of her friend the little red bird.

"Sing louder!" urged Mr. Murphy. "More oomph. Come *on!*"

Lulu and Val swayed back and forth, trying to out-sing each other.

The boys in the back row were even louder.

They made such a racket that Florinda and her angels-in-training had to stop their own heavenly choir practice.

"They're singing about us," bragged Celeste.

"Ouch!" Serena covered her delicate ears with her hands. "It hurts."

"It's the thought that counts," Florinda reminded her.

"Look!" Amber pointed to earth. "Even Rachel's singing."

It was true. After the class had run through the Angel Corners song twice, Rachel had picked up the words and tune, and now she was singing along.

"Sing louder!" Toby nudged her. "You have a great voice."

No. Rachel shook her head. It was one thing to be part of a chorus. Rachel loved that. But she did not want to stick out the way Toby did.

That was much too scary.

12

Whistling Teakettles

Later that day, Toby reminded Rachel of her promise. "Remember, you said you would sell lots of tickets."

"I will," Rachel vowed.

"See you." Toby hurried off to ballet class.

"Um, Val," Rachel asked, "can I sell tickets with you?"

"Sure!" Val agreed. "Lulu and I are going to go to her dad's video store. We're going to try selling tickets to his customers."

"Val just happened to think of it," said Lulu, "because she overheard Zeb Burgess say he's got to return his Super Nintendo game today."

Rachel laughed. Being boy-crazy seemed to take

a lot of energy and skill. You had to study the boy's moves like a detective.

At Starlight Video, Rachel met Lulu's dad.

"Go right ahead and attack my customers," he teased the girls. "I'll even put *The Adventures of Baron Munchausen* and *Around the World in Eighty Days* on display. They've both got hot-air balloons in them."

Rachel could see where Lulu got her sense of humor. Her dad was as playful as she was.

"Look!" Val pointed. "Here comes Zeb's brother, Zeke."

"Hi," he said, strolling over to Lulu. Zeke was older than Zeb and was already in high school. "Here's Zeb's Super Nintendo." He handed her the game.

"Oh!" Val's face fell. When Zeke left, she said grumpily, "This is the third time I've tried to see Zeb today. And each time, I've missed him. I even wore my lucky T-shirt."

"Too bad." Lulu put her arm around Val.

Only a few more customers came in, and Lulu sold them raffle tickets. Rachel could see that there weren't going to be enough customers for her. "Val, Lulu, I'm not being much help here," Rachel told them. "I'd better find another place to sell tickets."

"Okay." Lulu nodded. "And if you see Zeb, send him over."

Val poked her.

Rachel left the store and headed down Main Street. She stopped at Derek's newsstand to buy some gum. Derek was chomping away on a chocolate bar.

"I'm eating up all my profits," he joked.

Rachel laughed. Derek was so friendly, Rachel decided to try making *him* her first customer.

"Uh . . . Derek . . ." she began, "you wouldn't want to buy a raffle ticket, would you?"

"Well, if you put it that way, no, I wouldn't."

"Oh, okay." Rachel began walking away.

"But," continued Derek, "if you ask me in a more positive way, I might be interested. Maybe you could say, 'How would you like to buy a raffle ticket? You could win a fabulous prize!' And this time, Rachel, you might tell me what the prize *is*."

"Oh, didn't I tell you?" Rachel flushed.

"Come on," Derek urged. "Try it again."

Rachel took a deep breath and launched into her speech with oomph. "Wouldn't you like to buy a raffle ticket? It's only a dollar, and you can win a ride in a hot-air balloon, just like in that movie *The Adventures of Baron Munchausen!*"

"That's the ticket." Derek beamed. He handed Rachel a dollar. "See what I mean? Just be positive."

"I will." Rachel grinned. "Derek, you're my very first sale!"

"I sort of suspected that," he said as Rachel hurried away.

Her step was springy, as she wondered where she should start.

Rachel was trying to choose between the beauty salon and the fire station when her friend the tiny red bird came flying by.

It headed down Main Street, and Rachel felt that the bird wanted her to follow.

"Hey, wait for me!" Rachel rushed after it.

Suddenly, the red bird stopped, hovering in front of the kitchenware store. When someone opened the door to come out, the bird flew inside.

What are you up to? Rachel wondered. She dashed into the store.

Rachel looked around, but she couldn't see the bird anywhere.

In the window, she noticed a display of whistling teakettles and fancy teapots. There were bright, shiny kettles and pots shaped like hippos and big friendly cows. One teapot had Alice in Wonderland on the lid and the Mad Hatter sitting on the spout. Rachel's favorite was in the shape of a red rooster. His big crowing beak formed the spout.

Suddenly, one of the teakettles began to whistle. Well, it wasn't whistling, exactly. No! It was singing, *"Whistle while you work . . ."*

Rachel looked around for a loudspeaker, but

there wasn't any. The singing was coming straight from that teakettle.

Then the other kettles started singing! And all the teapots, too! All the customers in the store stopped to stare—and listen.

"I guess it's a special promotion for teakettles," said a man with an armful of kitchen towels.

On the street, a meter maid writing a parking ticket stopped and came inside to see what was causing such a commotion. Then she yelled to the firemen who were out washing the fire engine to come take a look. In the beauty salon, Ms. O'Malley was gazing out the window while sitting under the dryer and saw the firemen rush by. "What in heaven's name is going on?" she said. She and the salon's three other customers plus two hairdressers and the manicurist stopped what they were doing and ran across the street to see.

"It's a great pick-me-up on a dull afternoon," said a fireman, beginning to sing along. He called over all his buddies, and they added their loud basses and tenors to the din.

Soon everyone in the huge crowd was singing or whistling along.

Rachel joined in, too. She couldn't resist.

The music was so happy, Rachel sang with more and more oomph. She didn't notice that she was suddenly singing a solo.

At the end of the song, the crowd applauded.

"What a lovely voice you have, dear," said the meter maid.

Rachel blushed bright red.

"We all stopped to hear you," added the fire chief, beaming.

"Really?" Rachel gazed around at all the happy, smiling faces. It was kind of nice being the center of attention.

While every eye was on her, Rachel got a terrific idea. She shouted, "I have raffle tickets to sell—for only one dollar! It's a once-in-a-lifetime chance to ride in a hot-air balloon! And all the money goes to fix the angel clock."

"I'll take three," the meter maid said promptly.

"I'll take five! One for each of my kids!" shouted the fire chief.

The whole crowd was eager to buy tickets. Rachel sold twenty-two tickets in fifteen minutes.

"I'll take one," said a good-looking boy her own age.

"Zeb Burgess," the fire chief called out, "if you win, I'll never forgive you! Isn't it enough that every girl in town is after you?"

So that's Zeb. Rachel thought. *He is cute!*

A few minutes later, Rachel was alone again.

That's when she noticed the tiny red bird about to fly back out the door.

Rachel, Meet Your Angel!

"*You* did that, didn't you?" said Rachel, so pleased with herself that she felt giddy.

The bird shimmered a brighter red, sang a few notes, then flew out the door.

Rachel stood there, her mind racing. "That red bird had the same voice as the angel in my dream. She's my guardian angel, I just know it! Daddy was right! There *are* angels here!"

Rachel raced home. She was bursting to tell somebody.

But who? And who would believe her? She almost couldn't believe it herself!

Of course, up in the Crystal Classroom, everyone believed it.

"I should have guessed that Merrie would turn herself into a bird!" said Serena. "She's so flighty!"

"I guessed that bird was Merrie the first night she flew down to earth!" Amber said proudly.

Celeste ran her hand over her smooth black hair and fluffed up the ruffles on her gown. "*I* would have become a peacock! Zeb Burgess would have adored me!"

"You will all get your chance in Angel Corners," said Florinda. "But right now, it's time to study Higher Math."

Serena, Celeste, and Amber all sulked, hiding their heads inside their wings.

"Now, now, be angels," Florinda cajoled, and she recited the problem: "If an angel over Tokyo, Japan, begins flying in an easterly direction at four light-years an hour and a second angel starting from Kansas City, Missouri, is flying in a westerly direction at eight light-years an hour, over what town and country will they meet?"

"I don't know," Celeste joked. "But there'll be quite a flash when they do!"

Everyone laughed. Then the Crystal Classroom was quiet as each angel tried to find the answer.

Meanwhile, back on earth, Rachel was walking into her house glowing with happiness after her amazing afternoon.

"Rachel," said her mother, "I have a big favor to ask. Tomorrow, after school, I have to go to the McWitherses' stables and check out one of their horses."

"Is that Felicia McWithers's family?" Rachel asked.

"Yes," said Dr. Summers. "They insisted that I travel out there during my office hours. Do you think you can mind the office for a while? Answer the phone, and beep me if there's an emergency?"

"Sure." Rachel was proud to think that her mother trusted her so much. She had never let Rachel take care of her office before.

Rachel, Meet Your Angel!

Dr. Summers left to keep an appointment with a sick iguana. Rachel sat down at the kitchen table wondering whom she could tell about her angel.

Certainly not her mother—at least not if she wanted her to think Rachel was sane enough to watch her office.

Rachel wasn't sure if she should tell people. What if they didn't believe her? What if they laughed at her?

"I have to tell the Angel Club," Rachel said fervently. "Especially Toby. But maybe I'll wait until tomorrow."

13

Into the Woods

The next day was gray and rainy. The members of the Angel Club ate lunch together in the school cafeteria.

"I sold twenty-two tickets yesterday!" Rachel announced. "This is sort of wild," she began, leaning forward, "and you may not believe me, but I've got to tell you what happened."

Then Rachel explained about the teakettles and teapots singing, and about the red bird and the red-headed angel in her dream.

Lulu's eyes lit up. "It's just like *It's a Wonderful Life*, Rachel! Is your angel named Clarence?"

"I don't know," Rachel said, smiling, "but I doubt it."

Rachel, Meet Your Angel!

Val tossed back her hair and sighed. "I wish an angel would come and make Zeb Burgess notice me. Or maybe I need a cupid."

Toby looked at Rachel skeptically. "Just because you're dreaming about angels, doesn't mean that one is watching over you."

"Then tell me who was singing in those teakettles?" Rachel insisted.

"That's simple." Toby shrugged. "It was a tape or a CD . . . something like that. Angels simply don't flutter around in teakettles!"

"Mine does!" Rachel said.

"Right, Rachel. And there are fairies in the woods, too," Toby muttered.

Lulu said, "Rachel, you might as well give up trying to make Toby believe in angels. She has to see something with her own eyes to believe it."

"Right." Toby nodded stubbornly.

Val was more open-minded. "Mom says that people all over the world believe in angels. The next time you see an angel, Rachel, call me, okay? I want to see it, too!" Then Val changed the subject. "Lulu and I sold fifteen raffle tickets at Starlight Video yesterday. I think the Angel Club is going to outsell everyone in class!"

"Yesss!" Rachel cheered.

Toby patted her on the back. "You did a great job selling tickets."

Rachel was feeling so happy, she didn't notice that from across the cafeteria Felicia was watching her jealously with a vicious look in her eye.

After school it was still raining. As Rachel hurried home, she had the eerie feeling that someone was following her. Sure enough, when she turned around, she saw Felicia and Andrea quickly duck into the candy store.

When Rachel got to her mother's office, Dr. Summers handed her a sheet of paper filled with emergency numbers.

"It's a big responsibility watching my office," said her mother.

"I know." Rachel nodded. "I'll take special care. I promise."

"All right." Dr. Summers grabbed her bag. "Don't forget to give Hercules his medicine."

After her mother was gone, it seemed awfully strange. It was spooky being in the office alone.

A few minutes later, the phone rang. "My kitten climbed up the oak tree next door!" a girl's voice said breathlessly. "Could you come right over and get him down?" Then the caller hung up.

Rachel thought the call might be a prank or something. But just to be sure that there *wasn't* a kitten stuck up a tree, she went out to take a look. The rain had stopped, but the ground was muddy.

The oak tree was huge, but Rachel searched it from all sides until she was satisfied no kitten was in it. Rachel decided someone was playing a dumb joke.

She went back into the office to give Hercules his medicine.

She couldn't believe her eyes! The cage door was open—and Hercules was gone!

Rachel looked around frantically, but there was no sign of him.

Rachel knew that the puppy was too weak to walk more than a step or two. She went out into the hallway and called his name, but he wasn't there. The front door was open. Somebody must have kidnapped him!

Rachel ran outside calling, "Hercules!"

She saw fresh footsteps in the mud and followed them. The footsteps were heading toward the woods. Rachel swallowed hard. If she was going to search for Hercules, she would have to go into the woods.

She thought about her dad. He had loved those woods. Maybe if she remembered that, they wouldn't be so scary.

Rachel ran back to her mother's office and locked the front and back doors. She followed the tracks until she came to the edge of the woods. Then she took a deep breath and took her first steps into them.

"Hercules!" she shouted in spite of her fear. "Oh, please be here, *please*. Her-cu-les!"

The woods were dark and silent, and the air was still. A crow cawed, and Rachel almost jumped out of her skin. But she kept walking, calling "Hercules!" More than once, her clothes got caught on prickly bushes. Thorns scratched her hands as she pushed branches out of her way.

"Hercules, please be here! I'll never forgive myself if I don't find you," she said.

Soon Rachel reached a clearing. What a relief it was to see the sky again. "Hercules!" she shouted desperately. Tears began running down her face.

Suddenly a breeze blew up from out of nowhere, scattering a pile of leaves under a willow tree. And as the leaves rose up, swirling, they revealed— Hercules!

Rachel rushed over and lifted the puppy up into her arms.

"Are you all right?" She snuggled him. Hercules whimpered and shook. As Rachel comforted him, she noticed something shiny on the ground. It was a gold bracelet—Felicia's!

"That creep!" Rachel shouted in a rage.

She snatched up the bracelet and tucked it safely into her pocket.

"Hercules, it's a miracle that I found you!" Rachel crooned. "My angel must be watching over both of us." Rachel held the warm puppy close. Then she called out, "Oh, angel, I know you're there! Won't you please let me see you?"

A soft rustling answered her from up in the willow tree.

"Here I am!" trilled a high, light voice, and down flew a white-winged angel!

14

Oh, Hercules!

Suddenly, the angel tumbled down head first, landing upside down in the grass.

"Terrible landing!" she admitted. Quickly, she righted herself, dusted off her glittery turquoise dress, and smoothed out her slightly bent wings.

"I'm Merribel, your guardian angel. But you can call me Merrie. I'm so glad you asked to see me!"

Rachel nodded at her, too breathless to talk.

"You see," explained Merrie, her blue eyes wide, "I couldn't come in *this* form until you specifically asked me to."

"But you came in my dream!" Rachel said. "And you were the red bird who sang with me! You've helped me so much."

"I've certainly been trying hard." Merrie flushed with pleasure. "I've been training for this job a long time. May I have a look at that puppy?"

"Sure." Rachel placed him in her angel's hands.

Merrie began to rock him gently, singing a lovely lullaby. Slowly, Hercules opened his eyes. His white fur became brighter, and he raised his head. And then he wagged his tail! *"Arf!"* he said.

"Oh, Merrie! You *are* an angel!" Rachel gushed.

"Thank you!" Merrie beamed.

"Do you think you could help me with another problem?" asked Rachel shyly.

"I'll try," the angel said. "It's Felicia, isn't it?"

Rachel nodded. "She is so horrible! She could've killed Hercules!"

"The best advice I can give you now is to watch out. Keep your eye on her, so she won't take you by surprise. I can't do your work for you, but remember, I will be right there with you."

"I understand," Rachel said solemnly. "I'll feel better just knowing you're around."

"Of course! That's my job!" Merrie said. "Just call when you want to see me!"

Then she shimmered brightly—and was gone!

Up in the Crystal Classroom, Florinda applauded Merrie. So did her angels-in-training.

"Wasn't Merrie wonderful with that puppy?"

Celeste said.

"Yes," agreed Amber, "but Merrie could use a review course in Flyers' Ed."

Serena huffed. "*I* would never tumble around upside down! Angels should always be dignified."

Florinda disagreed. "Merrie has to do things her own way. Remember, each of you has her own personality and style. That's what makes you special." Serena, Celeste, and Amber beamed. They loved feeling special.

"Now," said Florinda in a stern voice, "has anyone figured out the math problem yet?"

Nobody had. So they picked up their silver slates and went back to work.

Meanwhile, Rachel was walking home, thinking about Merrie. She was absolutely out of this world!

The woods seemed friendlier now. Rachel saw chickadees and bluebirds in all the tree branches.

Rachel looked at a few tree trunks, hoping to see her dad's carved initials. But she didn't find them.

Back at the office, Rachel fed Hercules. Suddenly he had a humongous appetite. "Hooray for you!" Rachel cheered.

Soon, Hercules was running around, chasing a ball. He was back in his cage, taking a well-deserved nap, when Rachel's mom walked in.

"How'd everything go?" she asked Rachel.

Rachel, Meet Your Angel!

"Uh . . . fine," Rachel said. "Look at Hercules!"

"Oh, my!" said Dr. Summers. "I can't believe my eyes. Rachel, you're a miracle worker!"

No, Merrie is, Rachel told herself.

That night, Rachel called Toby. She told her about Felicia kidnapping Hercules. "And I have her bracelet to prove it."

"Felicia's getting worse all the time," Toby said furiously. "Someone has to stop her!"

"Right." Rachel took a deep breath and then said, "Toby, I have to tell you something. My guardian angel helped me find Hercules! Her name is Merrie, and she's got bright red hair—and bright white wings!"

"Oh, Rachel, you can stop all that nonsense about angels," Toby groaned. "Listen, I've got to hang up. Dad's calling me for supper."

"But Merrie cured Hercules! I saw it with my own eyes," said Rachel.

"Well, anyone who cures a sick animal is an angel to me, Rachel. Listen, come over after school tomorrow. You can tell me more about it then."

"Okay!" Rachel felt triumphant. "I'm going to convince you my angel is real."

Rachel knew just how she would do it: "I'll take Toby to the woods to meet Merrie. Then she will have to believe me."

15

Dancing with Michael Jordan

In class the next day, Rachel wrote note after note to Felicia saying she knew that Felicia had kidnapped Hercules. But she tore them all up instead of giving them to her.

Rachel was still scared of Felicia. She felt ashamed to admit it, but she was.

After school, Rachel and Toby headed to Toby's house together. Toby grabbed two chocolate eclairs, two glasses, and a carton of milk, and they went up to her bedroom.

Rachel had never seen it before.

"Cool!" she said. Toby had a huge poster of Michael Jordan on the wall. He was slam-dunking a basketball, with his tongue sticking out, as usual.

"I watch tapes of his games over and over," Toby explained. "I wish he hadn't retired from the Bulls."

"He's great," Rachel agreed.

Suddenly, Toby's eyes twinkled with mischief. "Michael Jordan lives with us, you know."

"What are you talking about?" Rachel asked.

"Watch!" Toby grinned. "Oh, Michael," she shouted. "Michael Jordan, where are you?"

A blur of gold fur came flying into the room.

When it slowed down and came into focus, Rachel saw a big golden cat. His round green eyes gleamed hopefully as he dropped a tiny ball at Toby's feet.

"This is *my* Michael Jordan," Toby smiled. "He can run and he can dribble!"

"And his tongue sticks out, just like Mike's!" Rachel giggled.

Toby grabbed a catnip mouse. Then she put on a tape of *The Nutcracker Suite*. She did a quick pirouette and then dangled the catnip mouse over Mike's head. He leaped and spun around, too.

"He's dancing!" Rachel laughed. Then she jumped up and pirouetted, too. "I've never danced with a cat before."

"There's a first time for everything," Toby joked.

"That's right," said Rachel. "Like a first time to see an angel. Come to the woods with me and you can meet Merrie."

ANGEL

"Come on, really?" Toby asked very seriously.

"Really," Rachel said, nodding.

"If this is a joke, Rachel Summers . . ."

"It's not! Come on, let's go!"

So they rushed out the door, with Michael Jordan close behind them.

They ran along, deeper and deeper into the woods. "I thought you didn't like the woods," said Toby.

"I don't want anyone else to see Merrie when I call her," Rachel explained. "Besides, the woods aren't as spooky if Merrie's around."

When they came to a clearing, Rachel said, "I'll call Merrie now." She cupped her hands around her mouth. "Oh, Merrie, this is Rachel calling. Can you come down right now?"

A rustling in a hickory tree answered her.

Michael Jordan gazed up, his green eyes wide.

And suddenly there was Merrie, sitting on one of the branches.

"See her?" Rachel asked Toby.

Toby shook her head. "I just see a hickory tree."

"Merrie, come closer," Rachel called. So Merrie flew down to a lower branch.

"Good landing," Rachel complimented her. "Much better than yesterday."

"Rachel, I don't see a thing!" insisted Toby. Her voice was growing angry.

Rachel, Meet Your Angel!

"But she's here. Even Michael Jordan sees her."

Indeed, Michael Jordan took a flying leap—onto Merrie's lap.

"Now she's petting him." Rachel grinned. "I've never heard a cat purr so loud."

"Rachel Summers, I'm never speaking to you again!" yelled Toby. "This is some mean joke!"

"It is not," said Rachel helplessly. "Merrie, why can't Toby see you?"

But Toby didn't wait around for the answer. She glared at Rachel furiously and then ran away.

Michael Jordan leaped down and followed her.

Rachel was near tears. "I don't understand what's happening, Merrie. Why couldn't Toby see you?"

"Because I'm *your* guardian angel," Merrie answered. "Didn't I explain that when I was here? Nobody can see me but you!"

"No, you didn't tell me that," Rachel said with tears escaping down her cheeks. She felt more alone now than ever.

"Oh, Rachel, I am so sorry," Merrie said, her eyes shining bright with tears, too. "I get so flighty sometimes, I forget important things. Florinda is always telling me to keep my feet on the ground and my head out of the clouds."

Merrie flew down, landing a little unsteadily. She put a hand on the girl's shoulder.

"Toby was my closest friend here, and now she is mad at me again!" Rachel sobbed.

"I feel awful about this," said Merrie with a sigh. "I think that maybe I should tell Florinda what happened and ask her to help us."

"Who is Florinda?" asked Rachel, her tears slowly subsiding.

"Florinda is the Queen of the Angels," Merrie answered. "She is a very wise soul. She'll be able to help, Rachel. Don't give up hope." With that, Merrie prepared to fly away.

"Before you go," said Rachel quickly, "how come Michael Jordan saw you?"

"Cats see everything," Merrie said brightly. "Now, remember to keep an eye on Felicia. I suspect she has more dirty tricks up her sleeve."

"I will," Rachel said.

Then Merrie was gone.

Rachel walked home wondering how on earth she would get Toby to forgive her this time.

Merrie reached the Crystal Classroom in two blinks of a star. "I made a terrible mistake," she told Florinda.

"I know," nodded Florinda sympathetically.

"You embarrassed Rachel in front of her friend," Serena chided severely. "You made her look like a mean liar."

"I know. I feel terrible." Merrie's wings drooped and she began weeping. "I let *you* down, too, Florinda, and you had so much faith in me."

"I *still* have faith in you," Florinda said softly, "and I'm going to bend the rules just a little bit." She enveloped Merrie in the warmth of her wings and whispered something in her ear. None of the other angels could hear it.

"Florinda, thank you!" Merrie perked up.

"If I were you," Celeste told her, "I'd rush back to earth this very minute. We're about to have a final exam in Higher Math!"

"I'm on my way." Merrie laughed.

"Bon voyage!" Everyone waved. Then Merrie flew back to earth.

She couldn't wait to reveal her surprise.

16

A Raffle Snafu

Rachel phoned Toby as soon as she got home. But Toby slammed down the receiver the instant she heard Rachel's voice.

The next day in school, Rachel wrote a note and put it in Toby's desk. But Toby tore it up without reading it.

When the lunch bell rang, Toby grabbed her books and dashed out the door.

"Why is Toby in such a hurry?" Val asked.

"Um . . . I don't know," Rachel said.

"Well, I can't have lunch with the Angel Club today," Val said, her voice sounding worried. "Mom called the school and asked them to send me home. She hardly ever does that."

Rachel, Meet Your Angel!

Rachel put her arm around Val. "I hope it's nothing serious." Rachel remembered the day her dad died. Her mom had come to school in the middle of that day.

Lulu went home for lunch, too, so Rachel ended up eating alone. Rachel was relieved that Felicia was nowhere in sight. The less she saw of her the better.

Val came back from lunch with tear-stained eyes. She passed Rachel a note that said, "Our raffle is off! Emergency Angel Club meeting at my locker right after school."

Rachel was stunned. What could have happened?

As soon as the final bell rang, she and the others rushed to Val's locker. Rachel tried to talk to Toby, but Toby ignored her.

"What's wrong?" Toby asked Val. "Why is our raffle off?"

Val's face was grim. "My mother got a letter from Felicia's parents. They said that if my mother gives away a free balloon ride, they'll stop bringing her all their travel business."

Rachel couldn't believe it. "But why? What's our raffle have to do with *them*?"

"They're jealous!" Val snapped. "Nobody is buying Felicia's tickets for the tour of their house. And everyone is buying *our* tickets! So Felicia's mother says if we don't cancel the raffle, they'll take their travel business someplace else."

"So, let them!" Rachel said.

"We can't!" Val's eyes filled with tears. "They have a lot of power in this town. They could convince other people to take their business away, too."

Rachel wanted to scream, she was so furious. She glanced at Toby, who didn't look back at her.

"So there goes our raffle," Val said, her voice trembling.

"And our Angel Club, too," Lulu lamented.

"We can't let that happen!" cried Rachel. "There must be *something* we can do."

"I don't know what," Val sighed. Then she grabbed Lulu's hand. "Come on. We promised my stepfather we'd help out at the newspaper after school. We'll try and think of something, Rachel."

Toby left without saying a word to anyone.

Rachel felt too awful to go straight home. She set out on a walk, hoping it would help her to think.

From his newsstand, Derek called out, "Why the long face, Rachel?"

She told him. "The balloon ride has just been canceled. You might as well tear up the raffle ticket I sold you."

"What a shame!" Derek was so sympathetic, Rachel found herself telling him everything. She told him about the dognapping and the letter to Val's mother.

"What stinkers!" Derek frowned. He took his railroad cap off and scratched his head.

Then he put his cap back on. "Rachel, have a Milky Way," he offered. "It will perk you up. It's gratis. That means 'free.' " Derek paused. "I've got some free advice for you, too. If you want to fix this, you're going to have to face Felicia."

Rachel shuddered.

"Speaking of the devil!" Derek pointed. "I see the blond, blue-eyed darling now. She's heading for the sweet shop with Andrea."

"Maybe I'll talk to her tomorrow," Rachel said, "or I'll write her a letter."

"Go ahead," urged Derek. "Do it now. Don't chicken out."

"Well, Merrie *did* tell me to keep my eyes on Felicia," Rachel admitted. The thought of her angel lit a little spark of courage inside her.

"I don't believe I've met Merrie," said Derek. "Is she new here, too?"

"Sort of!" Rachel smiled.

Then, before she could lose her nerve, she ran toward the candy store. She hid behind a big tree until the girls came out.

Felicia was holding a bag of double fudge macadamia-nut cookies. She had given one to Andrea but was gobbling the rest herself.

Rachel heard Felicia say, "Andrea, let's go somewhere else, so we won't be interrupted. Then I can tell you my plans for that stupid Angel Club."

What are they up to now? Rachel wondered. *I've got to follow them!* She winced at the thought. She stayed a comfortable distance away as Felicia and Andrea headed up the hill.

They passed the shoe repair shop. A few moments later, so did Rachel.

Toby was inside the store, picking up her mom's patent leather shoes. She noticed all three girls walking by. *What's that all about?* she wondered.

Then, to her surprise, Toby spied her cat, Michael Jordan, trotting after Rachel. He paused outside the shoe repair shop.

"Hi, Mike. What's up?" Usually, her cat hated Main Street. There was too much traffic. He came to her, and Toby crouched down to pet him. "What are you doing so far from home?"

Michael Jordan meowed. Then he sprinted up the hill after Felicia, Andrea, and Rachel.

"Mike! Stop!" Toby shouted.

The cat *did* stop, meowing and staring at her with his intense green eyes.

He's trying to tell me something, thought Toby. She set off after him. *They're all headed for the woods.* She began to worry. Toby still felt angry at Rachel for her childish joke about the angel in the tree, but she wasn't going to stand by and let her walk into one of Felicia's traps. Who knew what Felicia might do?

"Now *we're* acting like Rachel's guardian angels!" Toby told her cat.

Val and Lulu were in the office of the *Angel Corners Gazette*. They saw this strange parade as it passed in front of the window.

"Something weird is happening," said Lulu. "First we see Felicia and Andrea, then Rachel, then Michael Jordan and Toby. And they are all going into the woods. It looks like something out of *The Three Stooges*."

"Lulu, shush!" Val's face grew serious. "Let's follow them. Something is up."

And so they too joined the odd procession up Hickory Hill.

The Angel Club didn't know it yet, but they were about to have their most eventful meeting yet!

17

Up a Tree

"We can be alone here," Felicia was telling Andrea as they entered a sunlit clearing in the woods.

"That's what *you* think," mumbled Rachel, hiding behind a sugar maple tree.

Felicia took a large scarf out of her bag and spread it on the ground. Then she sat down on it. She took out her comb and ran it through her ponytail. As usual, her bracelets jingled.

Andrea sat down next to Felicia on the grass. She handed her a paper she had taken from her pocket. "This is an exact copy of the letter I mailed to Val's mother."

"It's a perfect forgery," Felicia cackled. "It sounds just the way my parents talk."

"Right." Andrea nodded proudly.

"And I could tell from the sad faces of the Angel Club that Val's mother believed it was real. She thinks my parents are going to stop using her travel agency if she gives away the balloon ride."

So that letter was a fake. Rachel gasped.

"What was that?" Felicia whirled around.

Rachel had planned to stay hidden, but she was so angry now, she came out from behind the tree. "That was me!" she yelled.

"What are you doing here, you little thief?" Felicia sneered.

"Spying on you," Rachel replied. "And I just got a juicy piece of information. I can't wait to tell my friends all about it."

"I wouldn't do that if I were you," threatened Felicia.

"And I may also tell Mayor Witty that you kidnapped his dog!" added Rachel. "I have your gold bracelet to prove it."

"You'd better not!" Felicia yelled. She jumped up and lunged toward Rachel. Rachel easily sidestepped her.

Felicia lunged again and Rachel began running.

"I'll get you!" Felicia yelled. She sprinted up the hill after Rachel. Andrea, who was not a good runner, took off after them.

Felicia was quickly gaining on Rachel. *I can't run*

much longer, Rachel told herself. *I'm almost out of breath.*

She grabbed hold of the lowest branch of an old tree, and pulled herself up. Rachel sat on the branch to catch her breath. Then she climbed higher, out of Felicia's reach.

"I see you!" hissed Felicia.

"Then why don't you climb up?" Rachel taunted her. "Unless you don't want to dirty your precious dress."

"Why should I bother?" Felicia glared. "You've got to come down sometime."

Soon Andrea came running up, out of breath.

"Andrea," Rachel shouted from her perch in the tree. "Why do you stay friends with Felicia? She's so mean!"

Felicia answered for Andrea. "Because Andrea knows I'm the only one in town who will be her friend."

"That's not true," Rachel shouted. "Andrea, you could have other friends."

Andrea looked up at Rachel with her big, sad eyes.

"She'd better not try," insisted Felicia. "I know a terrible secret about Andrea's father. And if she doesn't stay friends with me, and *only* me, I'm going to tell everyone."

"What's the secret?" asked Rachel.

"Felicia, don't tell it!" Andrea begged. "You promised you wouldn't."

"Andrea's father is crazy. He's in the loony bin!" Felicia said.

Andrea's face paled and tears began rolling down her cheeks.

"Andrea, don't cry," Rachel called out. "That's not such a terrible secret. My mom told me that people get sick emotionally, just like they do physically. Sometimes they need to go to a hospital so they can get better. Honest, it's not so bad!"

Andrea blew her nose. Then she looked up at Rachel. "Then why did Felicia tell me everyone would hate me if they knew it?"

Rachel sighed. "Because Felicia wants to keep pushing you around, that's why."

Andrea leveled her gaze at Felicia, who suddenly seemed a little nervous.

"Actually," said Andrea, taking a step toward Felicia. "My dad *is* feeling better. In fact he might be coming home soon."

"Great!" Rachel smiled, hugging the tree. "I'll be your friend, Andrea. I bet my friends in the Angel Club will, too!"

"That's right," a familiar voice called out.

"Toby!"

"Here I am. Your guardian angel," Toby teased. She was running toward the tree, her long braid flying behind her. Behind *her* came Michael Jordan. He leaped into the tree and settled down next to Rachel.

From her vantage point, Rachel saw Lulu and Val running up, too.

Felicia said, "Is this another stupid meeting of the Angel Club?"

"It is *now!*" Rachel shouted. "Listen," she told her friends. "That letter Val's mother got was a forgery. Felicia made it all up."

"Oh, really?" Val glared at Felicia.

Lulu leaped up in sheer happiness. "So we can still have our raffle!"

"Yesss!" Toby cheered as she shot her fist into the air.

"The Angel Club is definitely back in business," Rachel announced.

Felicia turned to run away, but she was in such a hurry, she tripped over a rock and fell down. Her bag tumbled open—and everything in it fell out—including Toby's drawstring purse.

"So *you* stole my purse at the flea market!" yelled Toby. "I should have guessed it."

"You can't prove *anything*," Felicia yelled back. But her voice sounded scared. She got to her feet and took off.

Andrea giggled.

"Way to go, Andrea!" Rachel cheered.

Rachel, Meet Your Angel!

"Rachel, thank you so much." Andrea smiled broadly.

"I'm happy to help," Rachel told her.

"I've got to get home, or else my mom will worry, but I'll see you at school tomorrow, okay?"

"Bye!" Rachel said, and waved. Everyone in the Angel Club waved at Andrea, too.

"Rachel Summers, are you ever climbing down from that tree?" Toby joked.

As soon as Rachel's feet hit the ground, Toby hugged her.

"I hope we never fight again, Rachel."

"Ditto!" Rachel agreed.

Then, from above, she heard a familiar voice. "Rachel, aren't you going to introduce me to your friends?"

It was Merrie!

"But my friends can't see you!" Rachel said, a bit confused. "Right?"

"I've worked that all out!" Merrie answered. "Trust me! I'm your guardian angel. I promise I won't let you down this time!"

"All right," Rachel said. "Merrie, I want you to meet the members of the Angel Club—Toby, Val, and Lulu." Then Rachel waited, holding her breath.

CHAPTER

18

Awesome!

And suddenly there was Merrie, flying overhead. The air shimmered red for a moment, and then she disappeared.

"I saw her!" Toby shouted. "I saw your guardian angel!"

"So did I!" shouted Lulu. "Oh, why didn't I bring my camera?"

Val's eyes were gleaming. "That turquoise dress was so elegant. I'm going to make one just like it."

"Merrie! How did you *do* that?" asked Rachel.

Her guardian angel landed next to her and whispered in her ear: "Florinda gave me the power. She said everyone in the Angel Club could see me—but just this once. She felt awful about my mistake!"

Toby was still standing there with a dreamy look in her eyes. "Rachel, I'm sorry that I didn't believe in your angel."

"But you do believe in her now, don't you?" asked Rachel.

Toby nodded. "Oh, yes."

"Mission accomplished," said Merrie. "Call me when you need me, Rachel."

And then she was gone.

"I'm going right home and turning this whole thing into a screenplay," said Lulu.

Toby danced around with Rachel, who said, "This is the wildest Angel Club meeting yet!"

Feeling dizzy, Rachel leaned against the tree for a moment. As she did, she noticed something carved in the trunk: the initials D.S.

"D.S.! Those are my dad's initials—David Summers. I found his tree!" Rachel beamed. "The same one that saved me from Felicia."

Toby grinned. "This has been an awesome day."

"And the day after tomorrow's going to be great, too," Lulu added. "It's Founders Day."

"Let's try to sell all our raffle tickets before then," urged Val. "I can't wait to see Felicia's face when our balloon goes floating into the air."

As the girls hurried home together, Merrie was already back at the Angel Academy. Something special was being prepared for her.

19

A Heavenly Salute

"Calling all angels-in-training," the Queen of the Angels announced. "Please come to the Faith, Hope, and Charity Auditorium for a special ceremony."

The heavens trembled as hundreds of fluttering wings answered Florinda's call.

Serena combed her long blond hair and made sure her gold gown was immaculate.

Celeste let the wind comb through her black hair and ruffly green gown. She loved the tousled look.

Amber came in her plain amber dress. It suited her very well.

These three angels-in-training took their seats in the first row.

Rachel, Meet Your Angel!

Suddenly the lights went out in the auditorium.

Florinda walked onto the enormous stage, her silver gown trailing gracefully behind her. "As you all know," she commenced, "an angel-in-training was recently sent down to Angel Corners."

Florinda waved her arm at the crystal dome of the auditorium. All the angels oohed and aahed. There, above them, they could see Merrie's trip to earth, as if it were happening again right in front of their eyes!

They saw Merrie appearing as a red bird in Rachel's dream and as herself comforting Rachel as she slept.

They saw Rachel singing with the teakettles and teapots.

And Merrie's crash landing in the grass.

And then Merrie helping Hercules.

"Bravo! Encore!" all the angels sang out.

Florinda called out, "Merrie, would you please fly up to the stage?"

A celestial spotlight followed Merrie, as she flew over the audience and landed gracefully on her feet.

All the angels applauded again. The tiny cherubs were the noisiest.

"To commemorate Merrie's first successful assignment, I am promoting her to Angel First Class!"

"*Yaay!*" Serena and Amber and Celeste cheered. "We knew you could do it!"

"And, as you know," continued Florinda, "every time an angel is promoted, she receives a new pair of wings."

The Queen of the Angels waved her graceful arm, and before their eyes Merrie's battered old wings were replaced by new ones that were bigger and silvery!

Oohs and aahs filled the auditorium, and then more applause. Merrie had never felt so heavenly in her life.

"I am also presenting Merrie with a golden locket."

Merrie beamed. "It has a picture of Rachel in it!"

"And now," announced Florinda, "there will be nectar and cookies in the Heavenly Hall."

Serena, Celeste, and Amber were the first to fly up and congratulate their friend.

"Merrie, you were wonderful!" exclaimed Serena. "I'm sorry I teased you so much."

"I hope I do as good a job as you," said Amber.

Celeste agreed. "I'll be asking you for pointers when it's my turn to visit earth."

Then they all flew off together for heavenly treats in the Heavenly Hall.

CHAPTER

20

Up, Up, and Away!

Everyone in Angel Corners was bustling in preparation for Founders Day. Ms. Fisher announced to Rachel's class that the Angel Club had set a record for fifth-grade ticket sales.

Everyone applauded except Felicia.

"I'm proud of all of you in my class," said Ms. Fisher. "You can all take a bow."

The class cheered themselves. Jimmy Nordstrom stuck his fingers in his mouth and whistled.

"See you tomorrow," Val told Rachel as they all left school. "I'll be wearing my new fringed jacket. Zeb Burgess will have to notice me!"

"I hope he does before you go away to college," Lulu teased.

CORNERS

Early the next morning, the members of the Angel Club hurried to the village green.

Huge green-and-white striped tents had been set up. All the stores on Main Street had red-white-and-blue bunting.

The parade began promptly at noon, with the Angel Corners High School marching band playing the town anthem.

Rachel sang along—as loud as Toby!

Then they rushed to the pet show. Michael Jordan won the "Most Charming Cat" prize after he danced with Toby.

Andrea showed her flop-eared rabbit, which won the prize for "Most Unusual Pet."

"Way to go, Andrea!" The Angel Club cheered.

When Hercules won the "Cutest Puppy" award, Mayor Witty said, "All the credit goes to our new vet, Dr. Deborah Summers! She saved his life!"

Rachel's mom blushed. She put her arm around Rachel and gave her a little squeeze. "Your dad was right. This *is* a great town!"

"Look." Lulu pointed. "There's Zeb! Val, go on and say something to him." She shoved Val gently toward the tall boy who was walking toward them.

"Um . . . Uh . . ." Val's face turned pink. "Look!" She grabbed Lulu's hand, pulling her in the opposite direction. "It's almost time for the balloon drawing. We've got to go. I don't have time to talk to Zeb Burgess."

"You know what?" Toby said. "I don't think Val's serious about this romance. She just likes dreaming about it."

Val giggled. "Well, maybe . . . After all, with angelic friends like you, who needs a boyfriend?"

Mayor Witty was on the main stage in the village green. "I'm now going to draw the winning ticket for the ride in the hot-air balloon."

The mayor stuck his hand into a huge box filled with ticket stubs and drew one out. He announced, "The winner is—Derek Weatherby!"

Derek looked astonished.

"Congratulations—and happy landings," said the mayor. "This ride is good for you and three of your friends."

"Um, thanks!" Derek said. Then he walked over to Rachel. "I have a small confession to make," he whispered. "I'm not wild about heights. Why don't you and your friends use these tickets?"

"Are you sure?" Rachel's eyes went wide.

"Absolutely." Derek smiled. "I'm wild about terra firma—that means 'solid ground'!"

So a few minutes later, Rachel, Toby, Lulu, and Val climbed into the gondola of the balloon.

"This is so great!" said Val. "See you later." She waved to her mother.

Rachel saw Felicia standing off by the side all alone. "It must be terrible not to know how to make friends." Rachel sighed.

"Well, *you* certainly know how." Toby grinned at Rachel.

The balloon slowly began to rise. Soon Rachel could see the whole town of Angel Corners shimmering in the sun. She was beginning to feel at home here! And Rachel felt, too, that her father was somehow with her, and he always would be.

As the gondola sailed higher, the angel clock began to chime. The girls counted seventeen *bings*.

Toby said, "Mayor Witty told me the town raised so much money the clock will be fixed really soon."

"I'll miss its creative counting," Lulu joked. She aimed her Minicam down at the town. "Wow! These are great shots."

As the balloon turned east, Rachel said, "I don't think Merrie is the only angel in town. After all, Derek was always there when I needed help."

"Hmm, that's true." Val nodded.

"And Michael Jordan, too!" Toby added. "He led us all to Rachel that day in the woods."

"I guess that means angels are everywhere!" Lulu said.

As the balloon flew over Angel Falls, Rachel said, "Maybe even Felicia and Andrea will find their own guardian angels."

Suddenly Rachel saw something shiny fall into the gondola. It landed with a clink at her feet.

She reached down and picked up a golden locket with a photo of Merrie's cheerful face in it.

"Oh, Merrie, it's beautiful."

Merrie's voice answered, "I want you to remember that I'm always watching over you."

"Thank you, Merrie." Rachel smiled. "Thanks for everything!"

From the Crystal Classroom, the four angels-in-training gazed down at the four founding members of the Angel Club.

"Hmm," murmured Celeste, "I wonder which girl *I* will get? Will it be Lulu? She's so much fun!"

Amber sighed softly. "Toby is fascinating. Maybe she'll be *my* girl."

Serena gazed down at Val, admiring her pretty dress. "Val is so glamorous. It would be heavenly if she were my girl."

Below them, hovering between heaven and earth, Rachel's friends in the Angel Club were also thinking about *their* futures.

Who will be my angel? each of them wondered.

And it wasn't long before everyone—the Angel Club on earth and the Angel Club in heaven—knew the answers.

The End

Fran Manushkin is the author of more than thirty children's books. A native of Chicago, and formerly a teacher and children's book editor, she now lives in New York City with her cats, Niblet and Michael Jordan.

Angels really do exist!

At least they do in Angel Corners.
And in the brand-new series *Angel Corners,* four ten-year-old girls meet their very own guardian angels—or, more precisely, their own guardian angels-in-training. And do they ever need them! Because for Rachel, Toby, Lulu, and Val, just growing up means getting into trouble.

Curtains!

FROM ANGEL CORNERS #2

TOBY TAKES THE CAKE

BY **FRAN MANUSHKIN**

The next day, things got even worse. When Toby came down to breakfast, she saw her dad grumbling to himself. He was sitting at his desk, paying bills.

"I have some bad news," he told Toby. "I've just written a check for this semester's ballet lessons. Madame Maximova was nice enough to let us pay her late. But she wrote a note saying she can't do it again next semester. She has bills to pay too."

"So, what does that mean?" Toby asked nervously.

Her father sighed. "It means that we can't send you to ballet class next semester, Toby. Your mother and I simply don't have the money."

"But Dad," Toby said frantically, "I've taken ballet for as long as I can remember!"

"I know." Mr. Antonio's face looked pained. "But we have no choice. We have to cut back our spending. All our money has to go to buy bakery supplies. Otherwise, we can't stay in business. If things pick up, maybe you can go back the following semester. Toby, I'm really sorry . . ."

Toby swallowed back a sob, then rushed out the door. She was in a state of shock. Toby hurried to school in a kind of daze. Nothing so horrible had ever happened to her in her life!

Toby got to school just as the bell rang. Rachel, Lulu, and Val could tell something was wrong. Toby's green eyes had lost their sparkle. And her feet, which usually danced restlessly beneath her desk, were totally still.

"What's wrong?" Rachel wrote in a note.

Toby wrote back:

"A catastrophe!

It's all about dancing.

I'll tell you at lunch."

When the lunch bell rang, the Angel Club rushed to the cafeteria together.

"Tell us what happened!" Rachel asked anxiously.

Toby took a deep breath. She first told them

about burning the bread and being grounded. Then she told them about how badly the bakery was doing, and about her ballet lessons coming to an end.

"That's awful!" Rachel cried. "I can't imagine you not dancing."

Toby's eyes filled with tears. "Neither can I!"

Rachel rummaged in her backpack and took out a rumpled tissue. "Here," she said, handing it to her friend.

As Toby dabbed at her eyes, Lulu and Val patted her on the back.

Suddenly Rachel made a decision. "Let's have an emergency meeting of the Angel Club this afternoon."

"Why?" sniffled Toby.

"So we can find a way to help you."

"But what can the Angel Club do?" asked Val.

"A lot!" Rachel's eyes flashed with determination. "We made money to fix the angel clock, didn't we? That was our very first project. Well, our second project can be Toby!"

"That's a great idea!" Lulu chimed in, running her hand through her persistently rumpled hair.

Toby perked up. "You are all such good friends!"

"Let's meet at my house right after school," Rachel suggested. "Can everyone come?"

"Yes!" Val and Lulu said together.

"But we have to make it a fast meeting," Toby reminded them. "I'm grounded."

"Okay," Rachel said. "Does everyone have enough apple juice and cookies? Good! Since the meeting's at my house, I'll call it to order. Does anyone have any ideas on how we can help Toby with her ballet lessons?"

Lulu's hand shot up. "I have one! Let's make a funny home-video and send it to that TV show, *America's Silliest Videos*. If we win a big prize, we can give the money to Toby."

"But what if we don't win?" said practical Val. "It would be fun to try, but I think we need to think of something closer to home."

Rachel said, "I have an idea! Back in Los Angeles, our school had a car wash to raise money for a girl who needed a brain operation. If she hadn't had the operation she would have died! Maybe we can have a car wash for you, Toby."

"Rachel, you're terrific to think of that," Toby said, "but my ballet lessons aren't exactly a matter of life or death."

"Yes they are!" Rachel said loyally. "I mean, they are to you."

Val thoughtfully licked a cookie crumb from the corner of her mouth, then said, "Maybe I can write about you in my stepfather's newspaper. I'm starting my own column this week. It's called "The Fifth Grade Insider."

"Please don't!" Toby said quickly. "Mom and Dad would be so embarrassed, and so would I!"

"But we have to do something!" Val insisted.

"Can anyone think of any other ideas?" Rachel asked.

Nobody could.

"I've got to get home," said Toby, "seeing as I am grounded."

"Toby, we won't let you down!" Val promised. "When the Angel Club is on a case, we never give up!"

As Rachel walked Toby to the door, she said wistfully, "Wouldn't this be a great time for your guardian angel to come."

"Definitely!" Toby responded.

"Look out for a little red bird," Rachel suggested. "Remember, that's how my guardian angel came!"

"I know. I'll keep watching!" Toby promised.

When Toby got home, she was practically knocked down by her older brother, Brian, who was rushing out.

"Hey, watch it!" Toby yelled.

"Sorry!" Brian blurted. "I've got to get out of here! There's a red bird in the backyard making an incredible racket. I'm having enough trouble doing my homework without that."

"Did you say a red bird?" Toby's eyes lit up.

"Yeah! A red-headed woodpecker."

"Brian, thanks! Thanks a lot." Toby raced around to the back.

Brian shrugged. "I always knew you had a screw loose."

"That bird has to be my guardian angel!" Toby told herself. She found the woodpecker right away, hammering on the trunk of an old crab-apple tree. It would have been hard to miss, with its bright head.

"Hi!" Toby waved at the bird, who ignored her and hopped farther up the tree. "Are you my guardian angel? Please say yes! I need you so much! If I have to give up ballet, I don't know what I'll do. Can't you help me? Please?"

"*Queeeeeek!*" The woodpecker squawked and flew away.